This book belongs to

For my

Mum and Dad,
Mary and Andrew

A DORLING KINDERSLEY BOOK

LONDON • NEW YORK • SYDNEY • STUTTGART

www.dk.com

First published in Great Britain in 1999
by Dorling Kindersley Limited,
9 Henrietta Street, London WC2E 8PS

2 4 6 8 10 9 7 5 3 1

A CIP catalogue record for this book is available from the British Library.

ISBN 0-7513-7169-6 (Hardback)
ISBN 0-7513-6246-8 (Paperback)

Colour reproduction by Dot Gradations, UK
Printed in Hong Kong by Wing King Tong

Hide and Sleep

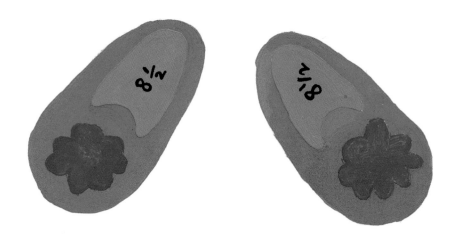

melanie walsh

Hello! I'm Poppy. I love to wear my crown.

It's my bedtime now,
but I'm going
to hide...

bye!

Pooh!
It's a bit smelly in here...

But the kittens
don't seem
to mind.

I just about fit
in here.

But Taffy doesn't think so!

Grrrr...

I know ...

I'll hide behind the sofa.

Oh, no!
Too many
toys!

Ah! That's better...

There's lots of room in here. And it's so cosy!

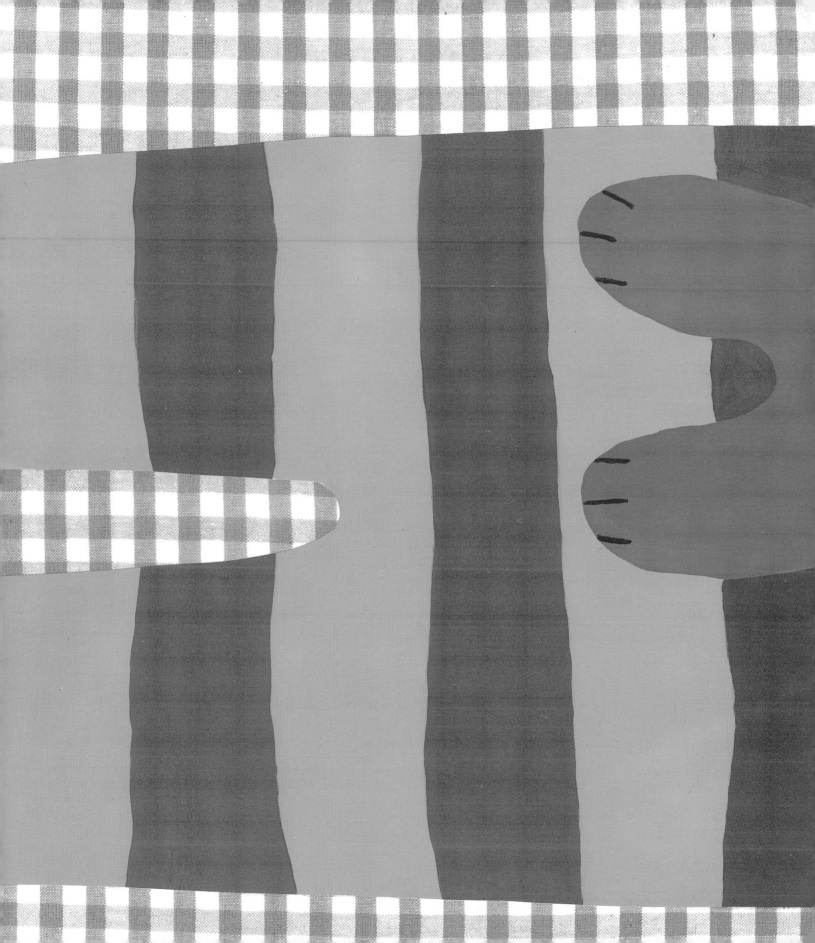

... for hours.

"Night-night, Poppy!"

Other Toddler Books to collect:

BALL! by Ros Asquith, illustrated by Sam Williams

PANDA BIG AND PANDA SmALL by Jane Cabrera

CATERPILLAR'S WISH by Mary Murphy

BABY LOVES by Michael Lawrence,
illustrated by Adrian Reynolds

THE PIG WHO WISHED by Joyce Dunbar,
illustrated by Selina Young

I'M TOO BUSY by Helen Stephens